READING CORNER

Percy the Postman

A rhyming story
in a familiar setting

First published in 2005 by
Franklin Watts
96 Leonard Street
London
EC2A 4XD

Franklin Watts Australia
45–51 Huntley Street
Alexandria
NSW 2015

A CIP catalogue record for this book is available
from the British Library.

ISBN 0 7496 5944 0 (hbk)
ISBN 0 7496 5950 5 (pbk)

Series Editor: Jackie Hamley
Series Advisors: Dr Barrie Wade, Dr Hilary Minns
Design: Peter Scoulding

Printed in Hong Kong / China

Percy the Postman

Written by
Sue Graves

Illustrated by
Mike Phillips

W
FRANKLIN WATTS
LONDON • SYDNEY

Sue Graves

"I love waiting to see what letters the postman will bring me. Best of all, I like letters from my friends and invitations to parties!"

Mike Phillips

"I live in Devon with my family. I love illustrating all kinds of books, from the shed at the bottom of my garden!"

Percy was a postman.

He rode a postman's bike.

He delivered lots of letters
To Bernie, Tom and Mike.

There were letters for Miss Holly,

11

And birthday cards for Sam,

A parcel for Aunt Betty,

14

And a package for Miss Lamb.

The school got lots of letters.

Percy took them in a sack.

There were cards and
notes and messages,
All bundled in a pack.

"You're lucky getting letters,"
Said Percy looking sad.

"I've never had a letter!
Just a card would make me glad."

"Poor Percy!" said the children
As into school they ran.

But Teacher gave a little smile.

She had a clever plan!

Next morning, very early,
Someone knocked on Percy's door.

Rat-a-tat-tat!

25

Then whizzing through
the letter box,
A letter hit the floor!

Percy tore the letter open.

It said: "We think you're great!

"So open up the door ...

We're waiting at the gate!"

Notes for parents and teachers

READING CORNER has been structured to provide maximum support for new readers. The stories may be used by adults for sharing with young children. Primarily, however, the stories are designed for newly independent readers, whether they are reading these books in bed at night, or in the reading corner at school or in the library.

Starting to read alone can be a daunting prospect. **READING CORNER** helps by providing visual support and repeating words and phrases, while making reading enjoyable. These books will develop confidence in the new reader, and encourage a love of reading that will last a lifetime!

If you are reading this book with a child, here are a few tips:

1. Make reading fun! Choose a time to read when you and the child are relaxed and have time to share the story.

2. Encourage children to reread the story, and to retell the story in their own words, using the illustrations to remind them what has happened.

3. Give praise! Remember that small mistakes need not always be corrected.

READING CORNER covers three grades of early reading ability, with three levels at each grade. Each level has a certain number of words per story, indicated by the number of bars on the spine of the book, to allow you to choose the right book for a young reader:

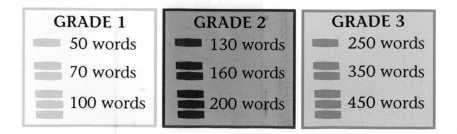

GRADE 1	GRADE 2	GRADE 3
50 words	130 words	250 words
70 words	160 words	350 words
100 words	200 words	450 words